HENRY HOLTON

Takes the Ice

by

Sandra Bradley

illustrated by

Sara Palacios

Dial Books for Young Readers

an imprint of Penguin Group (USA) LLC

DAD
HOCKEY
Mom
SALLY

Henry Holton's dad played hockey. So did his mom, his grandfather, his uncle, all twenty-three of his cousins, and his big sister, Sally.

The only person in Henry's family who *didn't* play hockey was his grandmother and that was because she'd hurt her hip. Before that she was voted MVP in the Silver Skates League six years running.

Henry's family was ***HOCKEY MAD.***

They were *so* crazy about hockey that Henry's mom drove a Zamboni to work, and on Saturdays Sally dressed their dog, Gretzky, in full hockey gear and put him in goal.

So when Henry was born, there was only one question: *LEFT WING or RIGHT WING?*

"Either way," said Dad, "by the time he's five, he'll be a pro!"

As a baby, Henry teethed on hockey pucks, and the moment he could toddle his parents bought him a pair of skates.

And away he went.

Henry glided effortlessly across the ice. He swished, swooshed, and swaggered. He didn't even need to hold his dad's hand.

"Henry Holton, you beauty!" Grandma hollered from the bleachers. "You are going to make *one fine hockey player!*"

But when Dad handed Henry a stick, something didn't feel right. Suddenly, Henry's feet were in a muddle. . . .

By the time Henry was seven he skated better than any Holton in history. But still he wouldn't—*couldn't*—hold a stick. And skating straight up and down the rink was downright boring.

Instead, Henry twisted and turned, weaved and wound. He swayed and shuffled and shimmied.

Henry’s parents were devastated.

His sister was furious.

Henry was a *MENACE* to hockey.

"Henry Holton, out of the way!" Sally yelled.

"You're ruining our game!"

And then, one day, it happened. Henry arrived at the rink for free skate, and there he spied a poster on the front door.

Henry asked his mom if they could go.

"Well," she said, "it's not hockey. . . ."

But they went anyway.

Henry sat in the bleachers, mouth open, heart pounding. The skaters below were like kites—brightly colored kites, swirling and twirling in the wind. There were no sticks, no pucks, no helmets or pads. Only bodies. Moving with the music.

One little girl, the same size as Henry, dashed down the ice, spun like a top, and finished with one foot high in the air.

It was *magic*.

ICE MAGIC!

And the magic gave Henry an idea that had absolutely *nothing* to do with hockey.

"Their skates are different," Henry said to his mom.

"Figure skates," Mom explained. "They have picks on the front of the blades."

"*That's it!*" said Henry. "I NEED PICKS ON THE FRONT OF MY BLADES!"

"Hmmm," said Mom. "Let's talk to your father."

But when they did, Henry's dad shook his head. "No way!" he said. "We're a hockey family, Henry . . . a *HOCKEY FAMILY*! You don't need new skates! You've got *top-of-the-line Junior Pros*!"

"But, Dad," said Henry. "Pros don't have *picks*!"

"Ice dancing is for *girls*," Sally chimed in.

Henry thought about that. "I don't think so," he said. "There were lots of boys there tonight. . . ."

But nobody would listen.

HOCKEY
SPORTS
TOP OF THE NEWS
BIG! HOCKEY SEASON

Deep in the bottom of his stomach Henry felt a lump the size of a hockey puck.

And for weeks, he benched himself. His top-of-the-line Junior Pros stayed in their bag, skate guards on.

He would not skate again until he had picks.

He would not skate again until he could dash down the ice, spin like a top, and finish with one foot high in the air.

"But, Henry," said Mom, "you *need* to skate! It's good for you."

"I need to *dance*," Henry corrected.

ROBO TON
H
X-BOT
HENRY
I ♥ HOCKE

Then, one day,
Grandma came to visit.

"What would it take," she asked, "to get you back on the ice?"

"I'm not a hockey player," said Henry. "I wasn't made for boarding and body checking."

Grandma reached into her purse and pulled out a photo. "Here. I've brought something to show you."

Henry leaned close and peered at the faded picture.

"*Wow!*" Henry whispered. "Who *is* she?"

"Who do you think?"

And suddenly Henry knew.

"*You* were a figure skater, Grandma?"

"Yes, a long time ago. But when I finally picked up the lumber and landed the biscuit in the five-hole with a mighty slap shot, well . . . the picks just had to go."

Henry could scarcely breathe. "Do you still have the skates?"

That night, Grandma met Henry at the rink, just as they had planned. She handed him the scuffed-up skates. They weren't meant for a boy and they were a few sizes too big, but they had *picks*! And Henry had come prepared. He'd brought three pairs of wool socks plus all the money from his piggy bank to have the skates sharpened.

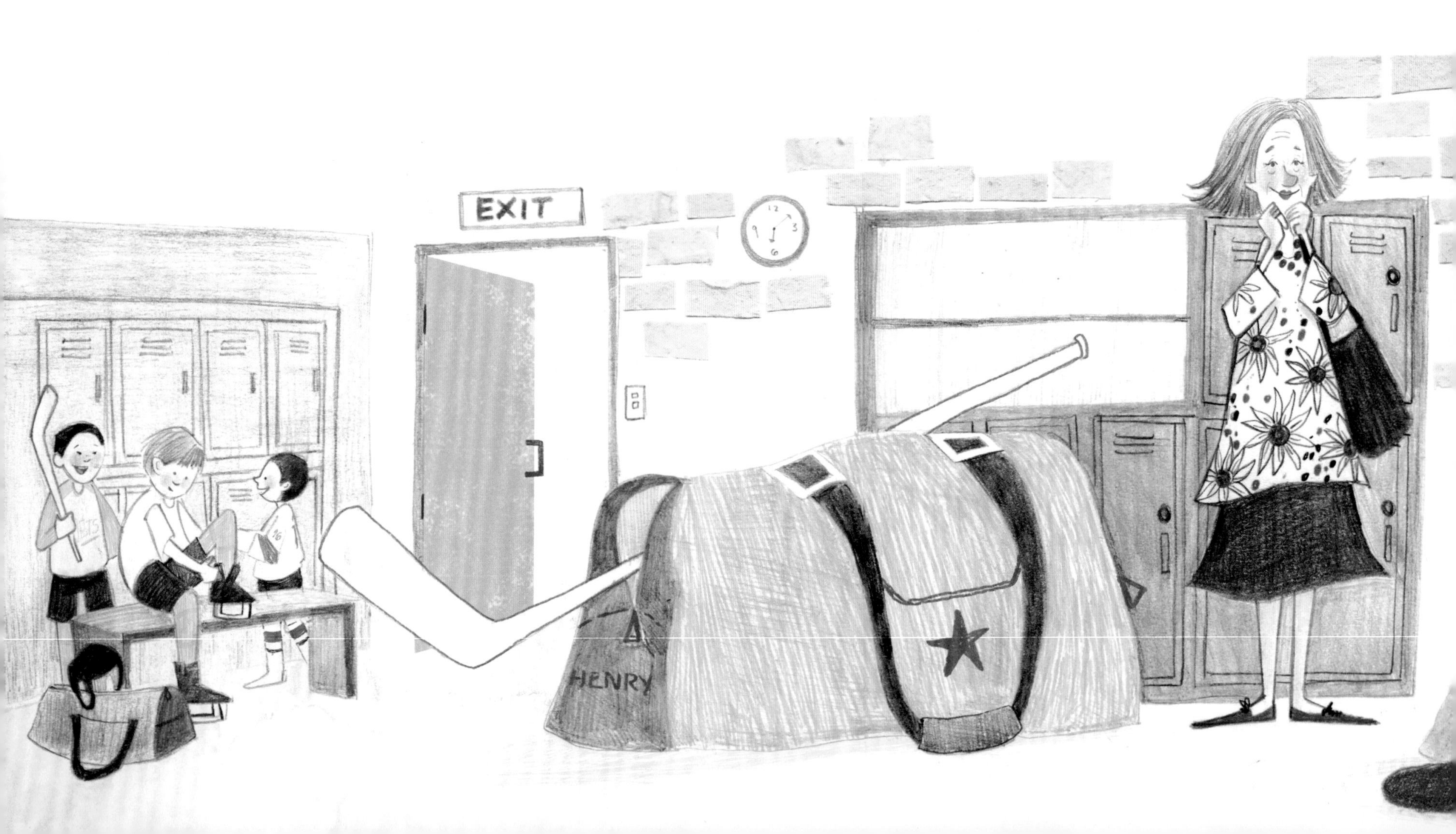

PRACTICE HOURS

When he stepped out on the ice, Henry's feet felt wobbly.

But he stood up straight and he skated. It wasn't his usual skating, and it was far from dancing, but it felt . . . *right.*

"Out of the way!" Sally yelled.

Henry ignored her. Henry ignored *everything*. Except for the music and except for his feet.

When the bell rang for the end of free skate, Henry ignored that, too.

Finally, the man who ran the rink blew his whistle three times and dragged Henry off the ice.

Henry's dad was waiting.

"Dad!" said Henry. *"Did you see that?"*

"Yes, Henry," said Dad. "Yes, I did."

The next day, when Dad got home from work, he was carrying a brand-new pair of boys' figure skates. They fit Henry perfectly.

When they got to the rink, a man was waiting on the ice. He wore black skates just like Henry's, and he smiled when he shook Henry's hand.

"Henry," said Dad, "this is your coach. He'll teach you all you need to know."

It took Henry sixty-nine tries before he could dash down the ice, spin like a top, and finish with one foot high in the air.

On the sixty-ninth try, Grandma was sitting in the bleachers.

"Henry Holton, you beauty!" she hollered. "I knew you'd make *one fine ice dancer*!"

Glossary of Hockey Terms

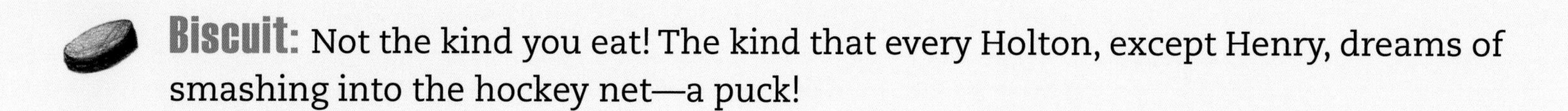

Biscuit: Not the kind you eat! The kind that every Holton, except Henry, dreams of smashing into the hockey net—a puck!

Boarding and body checking: Henry's idea of a nasty time. Imagine body bumper cars on ice. Minus the cars. Enough said.

Cross-checking: The Holtons do this with relish. Picture a band of pirates with hockey sticks for swords. You get the idea.

Five-hole: The gap between a goaltender's legs. The Holtons award a bonus point for scoring through Gretzky's five-hole (the tail block makes this really tricky!).

Left-wing and right-wing: Hockey positions—right or left, it doesn't matter, both are wrong for Henry.

Lumber: The thing that Henry cannot hold—a hockey stick!

MVP: Grandma's claim to fame—Most Valuable Player.

To my dear Samuel, Joshua, and Sarah,
you give me stories every day
—SB

To Ylda and Esau (Mom and Dad),
thank you for always supporting my choices
—SP

DIAL BOOKS FOR YOUNG READERS
Published by the Penguin Group • Penguin Group (USA) LLC
375 Hudson Street • New York, New York 10014

USA / Canada / UK / Ireland / Australia / New Zealand / India / South Africa / China
PENGUIN.COM
A Penguin Random House Company

Library of Congress Cataloging-in-Publication Data
Bradley, Sandra.
Henry Holton takes the ice / by Sandra Bradley ; pictures by Sara Palacios. pages cm
Summary: Henry Holton comes from an ice hockey–obsessed family, but despite his comfort on the ice, his aspirations lead him to pursue another sport—ice dancing.
ISBN 978-0-8037-3856-0 (hardcover)
[1. Ice skating—Fiction. 2. Hockey—Fiction. 3. Individuality—Fiction.] I. Palacios, Sara, illustrator. II. Title.
PZ7.B7256He 2015 [E]—dc23 2013049147

Manufactured in China on acid-free paper
1 3 5 7 9 10 8 6 4 2

Designed by Jennifer Kelly • Text set in Caecilia LT Std

The illustrations were made with colored pencils, graphite, cut paper, watercolor, and Photoshop.

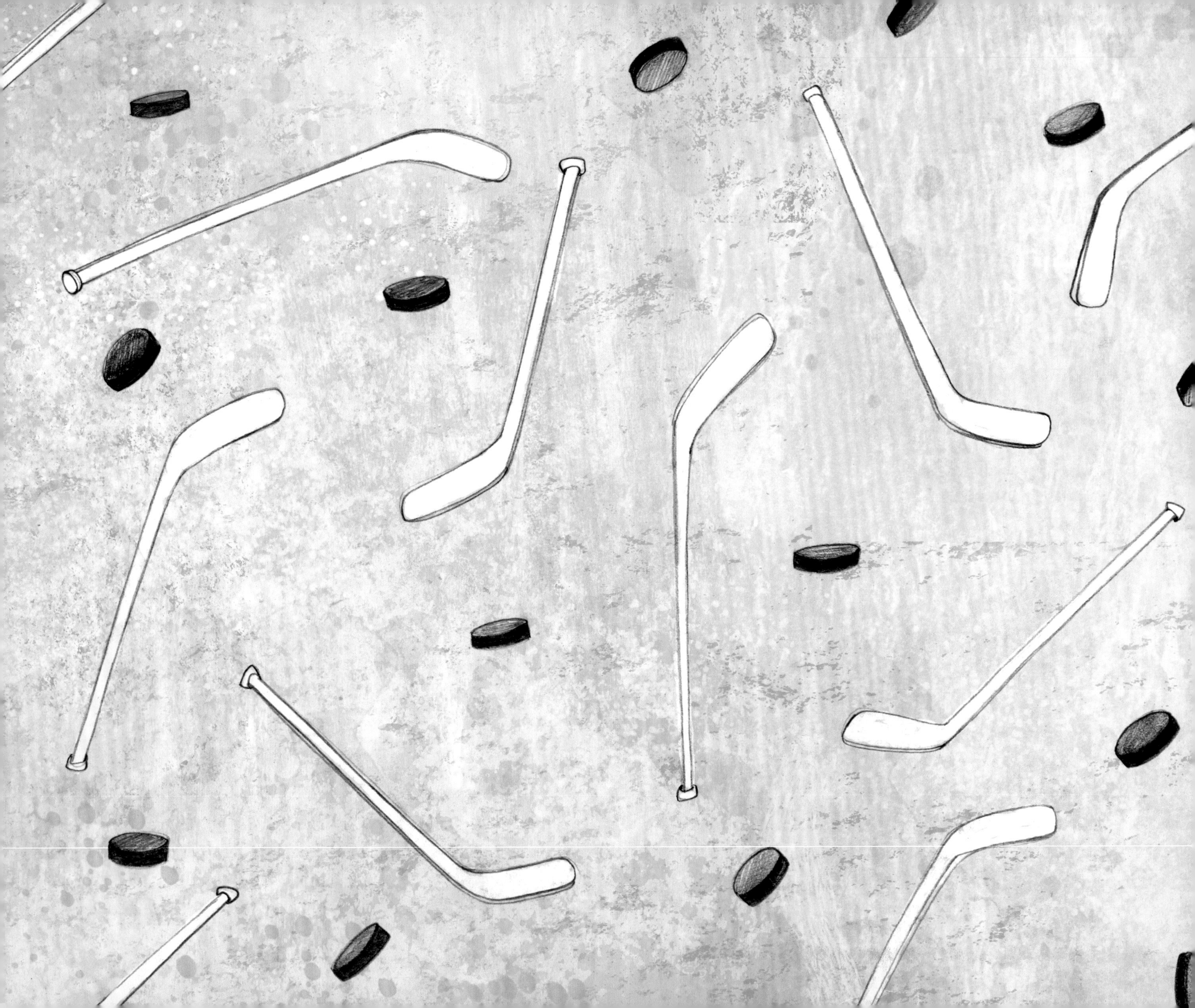